Shh!

Written by: Kala Holton

Dedication

To my amazing husband Randy Holton

Contents

Acknowledgment

To the Excel Book Writing and editing team for taking my

ideas and running with them.

To my family and friends, thank you for listening to all of

my ideas for this book.

Prologue

One Week Ago

Grace looked back at her nightstand one more time to check and make sure that she had grabbed her taser. You could never be too careful these days. She recently heard about some extreme incidents in her neighborhood. Thankfully, her neighborhood was safe. Grace headed to the front door grabbing her water bottle off the bar. She took the stairs outside of her apartment two at a time as she prepped for her run. Time mattered more than distance to Grace, she needed the hour cardio to keep her health in check. Grace has always been very conscious about her health and fitness. Instead of wasting her time into stuff that do not profit her in any way... Graced stepped onto the street and glanced around. It was 6:00 in the morning. The neighborhood was quiet this time of the morning, which is why she preferred to run now instead of when the streets began to populate more.

How she loved the small-town life. She knew she would never need the taser she grabbed, but she liked to think of herself as prepared if something out of the ordinary happened. She trusted people around her. She has been living here for years now, but a taser was 'Better safe than sorry.' Thankful that staying in a small town prevented the crimes she heard about on the nightly news. Grace proceeded to stretch out her muscles and rolled her neck, stretching out the morning kinks. Taking one more glance at her fitness watch, she hit the sidewalk in a slow stride to warm up before breaking out into her heart-healthy run. Grace was happy she was having her fitness time all by herself but she didn't know that she wasn't alone. There he stood in the shadows, across the street from Grace's apartment. Watching and waiting for her, he could tell that Grace was going to be a fun one. He was very clear about his decision for Grace. He had done his homework. She was perfect as perfect as he wanted her to be. The perfect number twenty-five. The jackpot. He left the way that he came from.

"I will let you go today, Grace, But I will be coming for you soon."

Grace was safe for now, but tomorrow would be a different story. Today was the day that he had been waiting for all month. Sure, he had taken twenty-three other women, but he had saved the best for last. He had been watching his last seven women all month. Grace was one of them. He knew their daily routines like the back of his hand. What they ate, drank, and even what they slept in. He chuckled to himself. There was only one that he really wanted under him, and he wanted her forever.

"Oh, my sweet, beautiful Grace. Daddy's coming for you, sweet girl. Daddy's coming."

Chapter 1

Present Day

It was a Friday night. The bar was full of women of different age groups as all gathered together to celebrate the lady's night at the Tavern every week from 10 pm to 12 am. Five buck margaritas every Friday were enough to bring the ladies of the town to the bar than usual and drink their entire stressed week away. It must have been one heck of a week for the ladies.

Only the elite members of the town were allowed to enter the bar at those hours, from 10 pm to 12 am. Those were the hours when the ladies were left alone to celebrate freely. Today the bar had a different entry. It was from a well-known, highly paid defense lawyer in the town. The entry was named as "Daddy." He chose to be anonymous but had the pass.

Daddy was a tall, young man around his late twenties. He wore a black, shiny shirt with his top two buttons open that flashed the upper part of his clean, hairless chest. On it, he wore a dark grey coat matching his pants. He looked hot enough for any woman to fall for him. Many even tried to offer him a drink, but he rejected all. He had other plans in his mind. Daddy was scanning through the bar, looking for his next victim. He knew his victim very well. Obviously, he had his research done. He was sure she was here tonight, enjoying her time.

It was only after half an hour of daddy's search when his eyes locked with the most transparent blue eyes he had ever seen. She had an average height, but the way she was dressed, it made her appear tall. She had a dusky skin tone with beautiful shiny black curls hanging down her back. She looked like someone straight out of the Disney movies. Her maroon-colored lips puckered as she laughed with her friends. As soon as daddy saw her, he couldn't control it. Her lips alone were making his blood rush below his belt. It was a feeling that was signaling him to call her over. He needed her to calm his blood rush down.

The blue eyes were constantly staring at him and then moving away. Daddy was the center of attention. Every woman had their eyes on him. She did too. When the eyes met again, this time, he motioned with his index finger for her to come over to him. Her first reaction was to point at herself as if asking, "Who? Me?" He nodded a yes. She did a slight nod of her head, telling him no, yet still smiling with her head facing downwards. She was probably nervous or maybe playing hard to get. But Daddy always got what he wanted. He motioned again for her to come to him. This time he raised a glass toward her as a silent invitation. His eyelashes lowered in a seductive way, teasing her, taunting her. Daddy has seen tough girls before. He knows this trick of his always works. The blue-eyed girl, too, stopped acting, for she now knew she needed him too. She couldn't control herself anymore.

She started walking towards him when one of the girls pulled her back and asked her where. She leaned into her group of friends and motioned toward him. even though they whispered, daddy could read her beautifully toned lips.

"I am going over to him," she whispered while pointing at him.

One of them said something in her ear that daddy couldn't catch. They all started laughing. She pulled away from the group and slowly made her way over to him, walking seductively. Her eyes said everything that needed to be said without uttering a word. She wanted him badly.

"Get ready, baby!" thought daddy.

As the girl walked up to him, she held her hand towards him.

"Sandy," she said.

He shook her and said, "Call me daddy."

"Haha, okay, daddy," she said seductively.

This wasn't the first time he had watched Sandy from a distance. He has kept his eyes on her from a distance for the longest time. Sandy was his victim. He would keep a watch on her to get to know about her. He knew what drink she liked, how she liked to dance, how and when she would buzz her head. He knew sandy more than she knew herself. Tonight was her lucky night. She was becoming one of the twenty-five girls daddy had chosen for this month's quota. She was lucky to get a chance to spend time with him, what every girl is dying for. Every girl fantasizes about a hot kidnapper.

He handed her a drink. He was sure that the sweet cocktail would be one of her favorites. Of course, his research was never long. Sandy accepted the drink. Her cherry red nails clicked on the glass as she took it from his hand. Her hand gently brushed him, sending electricity between the two. She looked at him with yearning in her eyes. He nodded at her as she tilted the glass to her lips. She closed her eyes as she took the shot and downed it in one swallow. She casually licked her lips. Her sharp nails were stressing him as she could use them to harm him, but he still remained calm. He reached for her hand as her eyes opened. He licked his lips in anticipation. The look in her eyes was enough to tell him that she was ready to go with him. He had to move quickly as he did not want to lose his chance.

"Shall we?" He asked her in his deep, sexy, and mysterious voice.

She grabbed his hand instead of answering and took him towards the exit. While exiting, she turned to one side and waved "goodbye" to her friends while smiling big. The way Sandy was acting, it felt like Daddy was a jackpot for her. She has never been with someone as hot as him. Daddy was happy as everything was going according to his plan. What could go wrong at this time?

While Sandy was waving at her friends, they started screaming. Daddy pulled her close to him. He wrapped his arm around her as they walked toward the door. The group Sandy was with hooped and hollered toward them, cat calls, and obscene noises as they walked by. He wished they would just shut up. The last thing he wanted was the whole bar to notice him. He turned his face away and nuzzled into her neck, nibbling on her ear that sent chills down her back as he tugged and nipped at her ear lobe. It teased the whole crowd. This made the crowd holler louder, but at least now they couldn't see his face. He could clearly tell how hyped up she was by now.

"Go, girl!" One of them shouted as they walked past.

"Save a horse ride, cowboy!" One of the older ladies hollered.

"He is hot. Let me know if you can't handle that. I know I can." Cracked the curly redhead with bright freckles as she threw her hips forward. Her words slurring with extra syllables.

Sandy smiled.

"Looks like everyone wants you," she said calmly.

He smiled into her neck as they walked out the door together. If only they knew what awaited her.

Chapter 2

While all the ladies were having the best of their time in the Tavern, Jessica walked in. Jessica seemed like she was in her late twenties, exhausted from work. She had her black blazer on that complemented her blue eyes and red-tinted cheeks. She had blonde, wavy hair that fell down her back. Jessica brought her files and laptop along, which made it appear like she was here to work. Of course, there's no problem with working and having cheap drinks. Jessica took her usual corner seat. It was unusually packed for the Lady's night.

As Jessica settled down in her seat, the bartender came to her for her order.

"Hey! Jessica. How are you?" he said.

He was a charming young man wearing a navy-blue buttoned shirt to match the exterior of the bar.

"Hey! I'm good. How are you?"

"I'm doing great, thank you for asking. How may I help you today?"

"Oh, you know, just the usual strawberry margarita, please."

"Right away, ma'am."

Jessica came to the Tavern every Friday after work to keep up upfront with the tough agent. This was the only place where she could be seen but not seen at the same time. The only place she intentionally blended in with the ladies.

The bartender came with her drink.

"Jessica, I have something to ask you," he said while serving her a margarita.

"Sure, what is it?"

"Why is it that you order this exact drink every Friday, and I pour it out every Friday when you leave it untouched? Then, you loom over those files until it is a watery mess."

Jessica's red fuller lips turned into a mischievous smile. It was a wide enough smile for him to notice.

"I will tell you about it some other time, Rick," she said with her face down towards her drink.

Rick watched her blush and smile. It was almost never that he saw Jessica smile. He couldn't stop thinking about her smile. She fascinated him, but she seemed so distant to him. Rick wanted to take her out, but she had always put up a tough girl attitude everywhere. He didn't know her story, but he would do almost anything to take the beautiful cop out for a fun night in the town. He was also somewhat worried about her health as she looked exhausted every Friday. She visited him in the Tavern. Rick knew she was different. She was not the kind of girl that usually visited the club and created a scene. She was more of a responsible, strong woman who held out her personality. He could look straight through her and see her character, her soul. He could sense that she needed someone to love her. He wished she would notice him and the feelings he had for her. He wished she would notice that the two of them would be perfect together.

Rick had nothing else to say to her. Her answer was everything. Jessica pulled out her laptop and opened the files of the ongoing investigation. She started working through it.

What am I missing?

How will I ever catch this guy?

Am I capable enough?

She started doubting her career choice. Her rank was based on success, and well, this case was going nowhere. This creep she is looking for left nothing behind. He is like a ghost. The same ghost as another twenty-five cases in her jurisdiction.

Where is this guy from?

Where did he vanish?

How will I ever catch a ghost?

All the entries were precise for each case. There was no data available about him whoever he was. Nobody knew anything about him. Jessica couldn't find a single clue about him. There were girls that were missing for days before they were ever reported. Most of them were last seen leaving the bar with a man, which isn't a crime or even a proper clue. No one could describe him other than as breathtakingly beautiful. Every other person had seen him in a slight flash that they couldn't even sketch him out. It was like he was Lucifer, God's most dangerous yet beautiful angel. Nobody knew about his motive. Was he actually dangerous, or was it just a mere coincidence for the girls to leave with this man? If only he was actually acting out as the devil. The further she studied the case files, the more motives she found, and the more the scenarios of kidnappings she found resembled each other.

This case was really bothering her. She could not figure out why? She was missing something. Something major. It felt as if she was missing the key to the case. Whatever she was missing, it nagged her in the back of her mind.

While working on the case, Jessica's mind flashed back to her 21st birthday. First, she celebrated like any other twenty-one-year-old girl ever would. Then, Jessica and her friends headed down to the beach for a no parent allowed weekend. They had the time of their lives, danced all night to Jennifer Lopez's songs, and partied till the sun rose. Jessica was happy she was finally into adulthood.

When it was time for them to head home, only Katie and Chloe made it back from the party. Jessica was not there. According to them, they searched for Jessica everywhere but could not find her. She had been missing for two years. Two years of her life that she could not account for. The world eventually assumed that she was dead. Even her parents had written her off.

Jessica wasn't aware of this. One day she somehow managed to reach her home. She knocked on her parents' door and expected a rush of love from them. She expected to be embraced by the people she loved. She expected a lot of emotions from them. Instead, she was cast out for not looking like how she looked two years ago. She was accused of being a fake, and even spat at. Her family and friends literally slammed doors in her face.

Her dad slammed the door in her face. That was the one that hurt her the most. She had no proof to show. She had nothing to say.

"My Jessie is dead. You just want fame. Or maybe you want what little money we are left with. It isn't going to work. Get out of here." He shouted at her behind the closed door. She stood with tears in her eyes. Slowly, streaming down her cheeks.

She heard his footsteps retracting loudly. He was angry. He did that when he was angry. She could remember when she was five, and he and her mother were arguing if she should study in a Christian private school or a public school. The memory faded fast. When the door slightly creaked open, she was staring into a pair of deep brown eyes, full of pain. It was her mother. She smiled at her. It was a smile little Jessie had never seen. It was as if she forced herself to smile while tears poured down her eyes. A smile full of pain. She invited Jessie in and took her to the kitchen with her. Jessie walked behind her. Finally, someone believed her. She knew she could count on her mother. It has always been her mother, her rock. Her mother gave her everything she could give her.

Only that her mother stopped at the drawer, pulled out her 9mm, turned the gun on herself, and pulled the trigger. It was a day that was engraved into her memory forever. Her father blamed her for returning home. But it wasn't enough that Jessica watched helplessly. It was something Jessica would never forget. It was something that her father would never allow her to forget. The pain from the memory stilled hurt to this day.

After being rejected, thankfully, Jessica remembered her account details. She had savings in her account that she used to get herself a room on a monthly basis. She worked hard day and night to find herself a job. She was determined to catch the man that made her mother kill herself. Her kidnapper destroyed her life, and now she was going to destroy his life.

"Robert Ash, I am coming for you," she thought.

After staring at the same set of files for a couple hours, Jessie placed her five bucks for the margarita on the table and waved her hand up at Rick, signaling her farewell. Then, she made her way to the door. Her margarita, just as Rick predicted untouched.

Chapter 3

Sandy had no idea what she had gotten herself into. She sat excitedly in the passenger seat. Daddy smiled at her. She was a busty blonde sitting next to him. He was getting hard but was waiting for the perfect time. Rushing things would lead him nowhere. While offering Sandy her drink, daddy had slipped a drug into it. He was waiting for the drug to begin with its effect.

Sandy kept on touching daddy's thighs as if she was waiting for him to make a move.

'I will have to do something,' thought daddy.

Sandy looked nervous yet excited about their time. Daddy leaned forward and kissed her. Her red-tinted lips felt soft and tasted like strawberries. This calmed Sandy. Her nervousness flew away, and she relaxed. She sat quietly with hands on her lap while daddy reversed his car and headed to the road. He waited for the drug to take its effect and looked at his watch.

'10 more minutes,' he thought.

Daddy reached out for Sandy's thigh, held it, and asked, "My place or yours?"

Sandy stretched out her hands, held daddy's face in her palms, and kissed him on his cheek while he drove.

"Of course, your place, baby," she replied seductively.

'Yes!' Daddy smiled at her and focused again on the road. He was getting successful in his mission.

'Only 10 minutes... I can do this... I have been doing this."

Daddy continued on the country roads. He looked at Sandy and saw her sitting calmly in her seat. He realized that the drug was slowly affecting her. He knew what he had to do the make the drug affect her quickly. While driving, he moved his right hand from the steering to her thigh. He could touch her bare skin right where her skirt ended. He slowly slid his hand inside her skirt, his fingers touching her. He could smell her. She was ready for him. Her wet panties were telling him just how ready she was.

He had to continue to play his part of an interested guy. His hand continued to the edge of her panties. The callouses on his hands caused chill bumps on her legs. A moan escaped from her throat.

He looked at her and saw her biting her lower lip. Another moan escaped her lips as her body relaxed. Her facial features relaxed, and her head fell to one side. The drug worked faster this way.

'Yes! Just in time!'

Sandy had finally passed out. After driving for a little bit more, daddy's turn came. Everything was going according to his plan. His main turn came, and he moved off the country road and headed to a secret route for his destination. Four hundred and twenty-five miles back to the little town of Arlington, Georgia.

Arlington, Georgia, is situated in Southwest Georgia and began in 1873. The railroad was a huge part of that early history. It was all that Daddy knew, having grown up there his whole life. He used to work in the fields with his granddaddy and go fishing with his brothers. His mama made the best pecan pies on this side of the Mississippi River. His pa would smoke a whole hog for the neighborhood at planting season when the ol' bores would come into his field rooting up his crop. The night hunters would give them a good ol' dirt nap.

His favorite memory was having church with the whole town on ma and pa's front steps, bellowing out Amazing Grace to a silent tune, slightly off-key. Daddy was from a big Christian family with Christian values and Christian faith, unlike Daddy. He was always running away from Christian practices. Not only Christianity but any other religion. He thought religions were very forceful. They were forcing you to follow them, and Daddy was a rebel. He would never do it if somebody forced him to do anything. The only person he was scared of was his dad. He could recall his father bellowing out his name when he wasn't singing, 'Robert Milton Ash!' and quickly, he would pick up with everyone else with the words of Amazing Grace. His father was the reason why he didn't like to be called by his full name. His father's anger was why he wanted to be called 'Daddy.' It gave him a sense of authority and superiority.

Such a mastermind, might have a weakness?

Anna. His high school love. He was ready to do anything and everything for that girl. Anna had the shiniest black hair he had ever seen and perfect brown eyes. Anna was perfect for him in every aspect, and he wanted to keep her safe. He wanted no harm to touch her and wanted her miles away from his uncle's trafficking ring. She was the reason why he would kidnap girls for his uncle, Adrian. Only so that he would leave her alone.

Even after him doing so much for her, he still couldn't have Anna. Anna did not know the truth, and he was an evil man to her. He was the one who was trafficking girls. If only she knew the real reason. The reason she could sleep safely at night. She could never know that he sold women just to keep her safe.

With his family gone now, he didn't have to worry about how they would feel if they knew what he did for a living. They left for a vacation one summer weekend, and he had to stay behind because he had just started a job down at the local grocer and didn't want to ask for off. His family died that weekend in a plane crash. The plane went down into the Hudson. There were no survivors. Was it the luck of the draw that he stayed home? Or miracle intervention?

He worked hard to keep the family's farm alive and make it viable again. He managed to do that and so much more with his full-time job and the money coming in from kidnapping the girls.

Daddy pulled into the barn. He cut off the SUV. Sandy was asleep in the passenger seat. With the press of a button, the barn floor shifted, and the SUV disappeared below the surface. On the outside, the barn looked like any other barn. When an outsider walked in, they saw just what you expect to see in a barn. Tools, hay, stalls, all the things one is required to keep inside a barn.

Robert was an Engineer. Since childhood, he loved creating things, preferably the impossible. He designed the barn to have an underground area. Almost like a living space below ground. He needed a place to keep the girls and stay off the radar. The girls remained in his possession for thirty to forty-five days under the cover of dark skies. Adrian would pull in to pick the girls up.

Daddy waited as everything settled. Walked around to the passenger side and grabbed Sandy. She was lighter than he imagined she would be. Her head laid limply to its side. Her blonde hair was flowing freely as he walked down the halls of the barn loft. The barn loft contained ten mini-housing units. Each holding its own toilet, small shower, and a small cot for a bed. It wasn't like the fancy hotels he preferred, but it wasn't the absolute worst either. He wanted the girls to be as safe as they could be while being in his care before they were sold to whoever purchased them. He made his girls feel safe, well, as safe as they could be. Even as their kidnapper, he still cared for them. He never touched them without asking for permission from them. He thought of himself as the guardian angel for these girls before the monsters he worked for sold them to the highest bidder.

Sandy never knew what hit her. He slipped the roofie into her drink when she turned her head. She tossed the shot back like a pro. Five minutes later, they walked out of the bar hand in hand. Honestly, when she is reported missing, the handsome man who walked her out would no longer exist. Wigs and colored contacts were a perfect disguise, but the best disguise was the makeup he used to create a narrow nose or a double chin. His own mother could not recognize him.

He left a bottle of water and removed Sandy's clothing, ensuring she had nothing to attack him with later. He had already taken her cell phone and tossed it out the window on the ride. He couldn't risk missing something. Even though the girls were hundreds of feet below ground, the chance of a signal being read was slim. He still preferred to leave nothing to chance.

If he was honest with himself, he had done this for so long he considered himself a pro. And what pro didn't want to retire to a larger city with more money in the account than he could ever spend? Only Daddy wasn't as stupid as his daddy always told him he was. Daddy was, in fact, a really smart boy. He kept no paper trail in any of his alias names. On paper, he didn't exist. No fingerprints, no pictures, He was his own ghost. He kept changing his looks so much that not even he could keep track of himself.

Chapter 4

Birthdays, a time for the celebration of life. Every year bringing in new beginnings. Everyone anxiously awaits for their big day to turn twenty-one. Jessica was no exception she had literally waited her whole life for this.

Jessica's 21st birthday was supposed to be an event to remember. It was supposed to be fun. Sadly, it turned out to be the exact opposite. A night of freedom that led to two years of her life being taken from her. Everything changed these two years while she was away. Her family, relatives, and friends searched for her and finally declared her dead.

When Jessica returned, no one believed who she was. Everyone refused to trust her or believe at the explanation she gave. Nobody believed her that she was kidnapped or even that her kidnapper existed. She was just like her captor.

A memory of the past. Nobody wanted to believe that she could have been alive.

The mind is a powerful thing, especially when something traumatizes you. Your recollection of events do not always fit into the reality of what happened. Jessica remembered what happened to her, well the way she believed that things happened. The details she remembered were unusual; she could remember so much about the man who kidnapped her, but never the details of how she was taken. She remembered the color of his eyes, the color of his skin, and most importantly, the way that he made her feel every time he walked into the room. The butterflies he gave her when he walked into the room. She would almost forget that this man, who made her so nervous, is her kidnapper. She remembered his smell, most of all, that was something she would never forget. The smell of sandalwood and eucalyptus with a faint twist of mint all rolled into one. It was a unique scent. She may never recognize his face again, but she would recognize his scent. That was something she couldn't forget even if she tried. The scents alone brought back a different time, a different place. The scent that gave her comfort but also ruined her life.

She visited different psychiatrists for this. To remember, to heal, but most of all to forget and move on.

"Are you trying to say that you are in love with him?" psychiatrists would ask, Not really shocked by her response.

"I am not sure. Maybe," she would respond, the same every time she was asked.

"Elaborate your thoughts, please," they would say. She couldn't give them what they wanted. They wanted details of what happened for those two years. But they were her cherished memories. And those she would hold close to her heart.

"You see, I remember so much detail about him. My memory is not that good. It's not extraordinary, but I still remember everything about him. I even remember how his touch would make me feel," she would say.

Psychiatrists had declared that she was suffering from Stockholm Syndrome. Stockholm syndrome is a coping mechanism for a captive or abusive situation. People develop positive feelings toward their captors or abusers over time. Nobody knew the truth. Nobody knew how much attracted she was to him. The truth was that she loved this man. She loved him so much. She missed his touch. She missed how he would always enter the room, take off his shirt, and gently touch her face. He was just like those characters she imagined in her romance novels. She looked so tiny in front of him. His touch was always gentle. It never felt as if he had kidnapped her. His kiss was gentle too. He was never in a rush, and it made it seem like he wanted Jessica to take his time. He cherished her.

While Jessica was madly in love with him and missed him, she hated him at the same time. She hated him for kidnapping her and making her lose two years of her life. She hated him for making her lose her family. She also hated him for giving her a good time and then letting her go. It was a love-hate war between Jessica and her kidnapper. She wanted to find him and make him pay for everything he had taken away from her. But most of all, she wanted to prove that he really did exist. She was waiting for anything, any clue that could just prove that she was kidnapped and he was. She, most importantly, wanted to prove his existence. She wanted to prove to everyone she was telling the truth and that she really was who she said she was. Most of all she wanted to prove she was forced to leave, that she did not just runaway. But finding Daddy was hard. Because according to everything documented he was a ghost and she was just a missing teen.

Daddy, you will not be able to hide forever. Your time is narrowing down. I will catch you. I will make you pay.

She knew she had to find him, even if it was the last thing that she would ever do. She wanted to arrest him for all the things that he did to her. Her and to others. But knowing she loved him would she be able to arrest him and walk away. Or should she hide him away like he did her and make him pay her way. Jessica liked power, and she felt that power could get her the answers she craved.

Even with Jessica's sexual feelings towards him, she would catch him for all the other women he was suspected of taking. She did not want to be selfish but wanted to punish an actual criminal. She wanted to act on her oath. These other women deserved justice.

One thing that troubled Jessica was that as to why he let her just walk away, and she deserved the answers to it. Why was she so special? Was there a reason she knew nothing about? Did he love her too? Or was there something else behind it?

Jessica was full of determination. She vowed to catch the man that she knew all too well as "Daddy."

Chapter 5

When Daddy pulled into the barn, it was no ordinary barn. It was well-engineered. Daddy had used his skills and knowledge to build it, whatever he learned while studying engineering. The barn loft housed the perfect trafficking setup. Nobody could think about something unusual that could be going on in it. Nobody could EVER imagine if anyone would be held captive in it. It was silent on the outside but filled with horrors inside it.

There were rooms where girls were held in for days. These girls were tied by chains to their beds. Daddy would remove all their clothes and lay a blanket on them to make sure they were warm. Each bedroom had a washroom attached to it. Daddy would visit everyone twice to help them with the washroom but still would not untie them. These rooms were engineered in such a way that even if anyone tried to escape, they would never be able to find a way out. Only Daddy could find his way because he designed it that way, just like a maze.

Most of the girls that daddy brought in were already passed out on the way. Very rarely, one might wake up from her sleep and would start fighting him. Then daddy would bring his hypnosis technique. The hypnosis technique is used to hypnotize a person and calm them down. Daddy would use this technique on girls to calm them down and put them back to sleep. He learned this from Anna's father. Daddy would also use hypnosis when the girls seemed to fight with the drugs, he injected in them. These drugs were not harmful and would only numb the girls' brains and put them to sleep. Buyers wanted the girls to be functional yet controlled. It gets harder to deal with girls that are uncontrollable.

Anna's father was the mastermind of this plan. Abel, a person with an angelic name but a devilish mind. A person who feared no one, but everyone feared him. People around the world, especially his clients, used to call him "Big A" for, well, because he was BIG and fearful. It was Anna's luck and Daddy's innocence that he thought about making a deal with Big A. The deal about Daddy kidnapping other girls for him so that Big A would leave Anna alone. He wanted Anna's father to set Anna free forever. But instead, Anna was found dead in the middle of the farm one night. It was three years of Daddy into his career as a trafficker when Anna passed away. He wished he knew what Anna was doing on his farm. *Why was she there? What was she doing here?* But with her untimely death and lack of communication with him, he would never know, but he was sure that her own father had something to do with all it.

Daddy badly wanted Big A to get caught for this crime and all he had done before. He took his love from him. But he also loved the attention and money the girls brought him. With every shipment, Robert would think about it giving it up. Then he would end up doing it again.

Tonight, his phone rang, bringing him out of his reminiscing.

"Yeah?"

"Big A wants thirty-five girls this week when he picks up. He said consequences were gruesome if you didn't make it happen."

"Gruesome, huh?"

"THIRTY – FIVE BY FRIDAY. I don't have time for small talk, D."

"FRIDAY? Are you kidding?"

"Friday, see ya then, sucker."

Argh! Adrian! He and his quota can go to hell.

Daddy would never verbalize those words as he didn't want to end up dead like the many he had seen over the years that worked with Big A. His life was simple, and he wanted to keep it that way.

Daddy wasn't sure how he was supposed to meet the quota with such short notice. He walked back out to the car for the long drive to grab a couple more girls. It would not be as easy as earlier when he grabbed Sandy. The bars were now closing at the time when he arrived in the parking lot. Ensuring to take the charger for this trip, he pulled out of the barn and headed toward the busy streets of Orlando. The place that never slept, with resorts, theme parks, and loads of bars. The best place for him to meet his quota. But how?

Suddenly he got an idea. He needed a group of girls, at least a group of three. Daddy decided to use one of his older tricks. One which would help him gain more than one girl at once. He would act as an Uber driver to kidnap girls in groups. He took out his "Rolling Uber" sticker and placed it on the windshield. Smart! Then he headed toward the strip with the highly populated bars. His app lit up, mimicking the Rolling Uber app, as customers requested rides. He laughed at the message about the number of people whom the riders were requesting accommodations for.

Parties of six… Parties of four…

"Come on, girls. Stop working in pairs. And just give me a trio."

He glanced up as three ladies walked out of a bar he was standing nearby. He broke out into a smile. His devil smile.

'It is my lucky day,' he thought.

He waited for the uber notification.

Ding!

There it was! The perfect number three! He accepted it quickly. He slowly counted to sixty, then pulled from his parking spot and entered the pickup area. The girls glanced up quickly from their phones as they walked toward his car. One had short, burgundy, curly hair with perfect makeup and a short purple Sequin dress. The other one had medium-length red hair and wore a long silver dress. The third one had catchy makeup done, had jet-black hair, and wore a knee-length navy blue dress. It looked like the girls had the best time of their lives.

He let up the partition he had installed. There was a speaker that they would talk through. This would disguise his voice just in case something happened, and one of them got away. He could still hear them through the glass. Daddy was a professional! He had been doing it for some time now.

The girls climbed in, laughing and giggling. Slightly drunk. They were drunk talking.

"Oh, you sound so sexy!" said one.

"Take us anywhere you like," said the other, and all three giggled.

They were taking selfies in the back seat of his car. He pulled away from the curb of the bar and headed south toward the resorts. He leaned in and pushed the button at the first red light, releasing the gas into the back seat. He counted to five as the girls laughed and grabbed the bottles of water every uber driver provided. They drank more, snapped more pictures together, and drifted off to sleep.

Between the gas and the sedative in the water, usually, his occupants would be asleep for the drive to Arlington. Today, the girls went to sleep quickly. Daddy hit the gas as he merged onto the interstate for home.

Daddy was feeling accomplished with his quick thinking to up his count by three tonight instead of just one. The perfect disguise in a busy town. *'I am so good at it,'* he thought.

The girls were completely passed out by the time they reached the barn. Daddy took them out one by one. He was not scared of anyone running from the car. He trusted his drug and his barn. Nobody could ever get out of it except Daddy himself.

Daddy placed each one of them in their respective bedrooms and tied them up with chains. This was the easiest part of his job. The medication he ingested the girls with caused rare side effects. The girls became unconsciously provocative. Grouping him, rubbing themselves all while their eyes remained closed.

The burgundy-haired girl was experiencing this reaction. She was grabbing for him, all while using her other hand to rub her breasts. Daddy smiled. Knowing how easy it would be to take advantage of her. He adjusted himself as he buckled her legs into the chains. Spreading her legs out.

It would be so easy to relieve himself, to relax her. He reached for her as she squirmed and moaned. He turned away, grabbing a blanket and covering the burgundy girl up. Switching the light off as he walked out the door.

Chapter 6

Jessica

Jessica was sitting in the conference room, listening to Agent Park as he gave updates to the task force. Another girl has been reported missing. This town is no longer safe for girls. The girl reported missing was Sandy. Sandy Waitcher. She was last seen at the Tavern in Whitney, Nevada. She had been missing for the past two days. Her friends reported that she left the bar with a male sometime at around seven pm. Seventy-two hours was the protocol to file a missing person's report on an adult. Her friends were at the local station promptly at eight a.m. to file the report. The end of their vacation coming soon.

When Jessica saw these girls, she couldn't help but think about how it would have been for her friends when she didn't return home with them.

Sandy's friends were anxious and scared. They were worried about their friend. Tears were rolling down their faces. The local Police Department called Jessica immediately as the motive of her investigation matched with four other girls in the same town. It is Las Vegas. Men and Women party here every night. Friday nights are specifically for women. What happens in the bar and after the bar party remains in Las Vegas. A woman might accompany a man back to his hotel to spend the rest of the night with him. Who knows what happens at the hotel?

Las Vegas is also known as the sin city. Lately, more girls have been going missing. They leave with handsome boys but never return.

"Jessica, I want you to begin with your investigation by interviewing Sandy's friends," said the head officer.

"Yes, sir!" said Jessica. She was scared to go through the mental trauma, but she had to. She had no other choice.

The Local Police Department separated the girls into different interview rooms. Jessica started with what appeared to be the head of the girls' group. She seemed to have the air of a boss about her personality. It appeared to Jessica that the other girls were just followers. The boss girl knew more than the other girls in the group.

The interrogation began.

"Morning. I am Agent Lee. This is my partner, Agent Murphy. We would like to ask you a few questions regarding your friend Sandy?" said Jessica.

"I have already told the other officer everything. So, I don't think there are any more questions left."

"We know you think that you have told us everything, but we need the details that you don't remember right off," responded Jessica.

"Do I need an attorney?"

"That is completely up to you, ma'am. But you are not under arrest. We are just trying to get an idea of what happened the night Sandy went missing and if there is anything that you may remember that stands out. So, we can find your friend," responded Agent Murphy.

Lee and Murphy stood by the door, waiting for her to ask for her attorney again. If she did, this could take a while, and every minute counted for Sandy.

The girl thought for a few minutes and then finally said, "You can ask me whatever. Just find Sandy."

"Let's start with your name."

"Carly. Carly Whiton."

"So, Carly, when was the last time you saw your friend?" asked Agent Murphy.

"Friday night. She left the bar with a man that looked three or four years older than us."

"Can you specify the details of his features for our experts to draw?" asked Agent Murphy.

"I am afraid I won't be able to do it. The man stood far away from me to notice his details."

"There must be something," said Agent Murphy.

"I am telling you, I don't know."

"Are you hiding something from us?" asked Agent Murphy doubtfully. He wanted to push her to remember to tell them everything surrounding Sandy's disappearance.

"WHAT? Why would you even say that? I was the one who filed the complaint."

"Sometimes things we think are irrelevant are actually just what the police need to solve the case. So please think. I want to save your friend," said Agent Murphy.

"I DON'T REMEMBER!!"

Carly screamed at the top of her lungs. That's when Jessica jumped in and tried to handle the situation. In no way she wanted Carly to call her attorney.

"Wait! Wait! Carly, calm down, please. Agent Murphy, let's not pressure her."

Agent Murphy understood what Jessica meant.

"See, Carly, there are a lot of kidnappings happening around lately. The girls leave the place of sight with a handsome man and then never return. We just need more and more information to find Sandy quickly," said Jessica.

"I already told you everything. What else is left?"

"The families of these missing girls noticed about someone keeping a watch over them. Friends have to say, the men these girls left with knew a lot about them. From their favorite flowers to their favorite drinks."

"YES! RIGHT! THAT'S IT!" screamed Carly.

"What?"

"You say someone was watching them?"

Both the agents nodded.

"I knew it! I knew someone was watching Sandy."

"You did?"

"Yes! There was a guy I spotted several times whenever I was around Sandy. He would even try to disguise his look, but I would still be able to pick out. I mentioned him to Sandy many times, but she was just too carefree to notice and always believed the good in everyone."

Both the agents were shocked at Carly's nonchalant attitude.

"Now I know why the guy looked very familiar. The guy she left with," continued Carly. "When Sandy didn't return, I just had it in my sixth sense that something was wrong. I wanted to complain then and there, but I had to wait for the 72-hour protocol."

Carly started crying. Jessica stood up from her chair and patted Carly on the back to comfort her.

"It is all my fault. I kept asking Sandy not to go to him. He looked weirdly familiar. She didn't listen. She always thinks everyone is good around her. Doesn't listen. Look now, what has she done to herself. It is all my fault. I failed to convince her."

"It's okay, Carly. Don't blame yourself. It was not your fault. It is not even Sandy's fault. I have heard the man is very handsome to resist," said Jessica.

"I don't know. I was just able to recognize him but could not remember where I saw him."

"Let's take our investigation a step further," said Agent Murphy. "Carly, you will have to help us to find your friend."

"Sure. I am all up to find my friend."

"I am going to send in a sketch artist. Try to remember what he looked like. Just close your eyes and describe what you see."

"I will give it my best shot."

Agent Murphy smiled. Agent Lee patted Carly on the shoulder.

"Thank you for your help."

"You and her friends can leave after you are done with the sketch artist." Agent Murphy flashed a smile at

Carly, hoping that the ice-cold fear that ran in his blood didn't show on his face. He knew that the chance of finding Sandy alive was slim. But there was no way he would tell Carly or the others that. They would try to find her alive, but they only had 60 hours left with that chance.

Chapter 7

Pulling into the gates of his country home, Daddy glanced back at the girls. They remained unconscious. The sun was beginning to rise over the horizon. Daddy was tired, but he still had so much to do.

Hitting the switch, the car began. It descended to the basement. Daddy proceeded with the syringe and filled it with midazolam. Midazolam helps make the girls feel dizzy and go to sleep. Daddy opened the back door, leaning over and injecting each girl with 1cc of the drug. This would keep them out, at least until he got them settled.

Daddy slung one of the girls over his shoulder, a method he had done hundreds of times before. The girl stiffened as if to fight back. Daddy grew tense, yet as the drug settled into her bloodstream, his muscles relaxed as she did against him.

He begins walking down the corridor, counting the rooms on both the right and the left. The basement held twenty-one rooms, with the hallway ending in a doorway. Each room housed four girls. He tried to keep them separated and only placed girls that were not familiar with each other together. He had learned that keeping them separate from those which they knew gave them a sense of insecurity, and he needed that advantage. Surely the girls were locked away, chained to beds and walls. But one could never be too sure in this line of work.

The room on end housed what he liked to consider his guest bedroom. The walls were painted a rich red that could be mistaken as burgundy in color. It contrasted the black poster-style bed that held chains and belts on the four posts. This room was especially for his buyers should anyone need a moment of privacy with the girls.

Daddy carefully laid the girl in the ninth room on the left and repeated the process with the other two girls, only placing them in separate rooms for his safety. He removed their clothing and chained them with cuffs to the bed, their bodies stretched in an X shape pattern.

This was the part that he felt so guilty over. He wanted them to feel safe and cared for, and as nuts, as it sounded, he even wanted them to feel loved. When just the irony of that thought was enough to send someone over the edge.

He grabbed their food and water and went into each of the rooms. He placed their food on the table. The newest girls from tonight would not be fed till much later. He wanted to make sure that they were weak enough before feeding them. Even a little bit of energy can get concerning for him. The other girls were allowed. One by one, they would be unchained to eat and use the facilities.

Daddy got back into the car and pressed the button to ascend to the top floor of the barn again. The sun had broken through the trees and was shining bright, bringing the temperature of the day into the mid-eighties. The morning was still young, but he knew it was too late for him to go to bed. He drove up to the main house pulling into the garage. The doors rolled up, and he parked the car. Getting out, he locked the doors and let the garage door down. He had meetings scheduled today with other attorneys. Lucky for him, his meetings were able to be conducted from the privacy of his own home. Things were not always this convenient, but he would consider it a win today.

Chapter 8

Jessica

The case about the missing girl was under investigation. All the agents were working effortlessly on the case. Jessica was looking at this case with her eagle eyes. Gradually, she began to realize that this case was similar to her past. Jessica always kept her personal life separate from her work life. But, if this imaginary connection was real, she was no longer able to keep them separate. She kept on going deeper and deeper into the case, finally, after connecting all of the dots of the case file and the file of her case that she carried in her head. She could clearly see that this was the work of the same man from her past. The events when she went missing for two years, the same events are now happening with the girls that are reported missing.

Jessica left with a guy from her birthday party. Just like all of these current missing girls. Her mind flashed back to those days two years ago. His eyes were of dark brown color. Not the contacts he wore to disguise himself, but his real eye color was so dark they were like looking into a pool of darkness. With all this going around, she decides to go undercover. She knew that what she was going to do was very dangerous, and it might cause her some trouble, but she considered this an act of need. It was now important for someone to take this step and figure out everything.

Jessica decided to discuss her idea with her director.

"What the hell? How did you even come up with such an idea?" He responded.

"Sir, this is the only way we can figure it out."

"I assume you just want to party undercover and have sex with handsome boys in the name of investigation."

"I assume somebody is filling your pockets to not let us dig into the investigation."

The director went shocked by this response of hers. It was an unexpected answer from her. Jessica was never one to shoot a short blow, especially not one about politics.

"Fine, Jessica. You can go undercover, but don't let me regret this." The director slammed the folder down on the table as he stormed out of the office.

Jessica gave a smirk and went to her partner assigned to the investigation. Agent Murphy. She tells him everything about why it is important for her to go undercover.

Her partner corners her. Placing his hands on his hips, his face was calm and collected, full of determination to change her mind. He was thinking of excuses to say.

"Jessica, you can't do this."

"I have to. It is the only way to catch this guy."

"We both know why you can't do this."

"Shh! Lower your voice. Only the two of us know. We have been partners for years. You know I can do this."

Jessica could not understand anything. Why would anyone not want her to do this? But she knew she could handle this. She could go undercover and catch the man that her team would eventually call Daddy. Just like she did.

"Jessica, listen to me. There are a lot of similarities to your case when you were younger and went missing. I didn't want to tell you. I know this is hard."

Her partner took a deep breath. Before he continued.

"Jessica, you cannot go undercover. If he recognizes you, you will be in danger."

That was it. She ran her fingers through her hair with a gaze like she knew it! There it was in plain sight. The connection she was missing! Even Agent Murphy was now able to figure it out. This was the validation she needed. This was everything she needed.

All the recent missing incidents happening in town were the work of Robert Ash, known as "Daddy" by his victims. She was the only one to have ever gotten away with making his name known to the world.

Daddy was Robert Milton Ash. Robert Milton Ash was Daddy.

Jessica hated him and loved him at the same time. Her partner was right. If he recognized her, she would be in serious danger. She didn't realize the consequences of her decision.

On the spot, Jessica decided to appear strong and resilient to her partner. Only this way would it be helpful for her to convince her bosses that this was the only way to expose the kidnapper and bring him into broad daylight.

"This does nothing to change my mind. It just makes me want to catch this guy even more."

"Jessica, you can't. This is not safe."

"Agent Murphy, I will do this," She whispered to him. "Don't fight me on this."

Jessica pleads for him to keep quiet with her eyes. As she flashed back to the day, she woke up shackled to the bed by her hands. Her feet were pulled together and chained. A homemade quilt was laid over her to cover her exposed body. The whimpers and cries of the other girls also in the room scared her and comforted her at the same time.

The memory soon faded. Jessica had chills in her arms, and her heart was racing. She was astonished at how much she remembered every single detail of Robert or 'Daddy.' She remembered his voice, his face, his touch, even his smell. She loved him more than she hated him. She wanted him, but on the other side, she also wanted to take revenge on him for ruining her life.

She looked again at her partner facing downwards.

"I have to do this," she murmured.

He looked at her with compassion in his eyes. "Jess, please."

"I'm sorry, I have to," Jessica states as she walks away to begin the chore of being an undercover agent.

"Jess, stop. Think about this. Don't do this. We can figure out another way to catch this guy."

His voice trailed behind her as Jessica walked out of their tiny office.

Agent Murphy was torn about allowing Jessica to walk into this undercover gig without anyone to back her. He looked at the director.

"I'd like permission to go undercover with Jessica. As a backup, sir."

"What are you waiting on, Murphy? She going to leave you out in the dust if you don't get going."

"Thanks, sir."

Murphy headed out the door right behind Jessica. If only Jessica knew how much he loved her and cared for her. How he understood how disturbed her life was after being kidnapped and coming home to her parents not welcoming her with open arms. Jessica was his priority, and he would do everything in his power to keep her safe. He loved her more than his partner on the force. He hoped that he could ask her out on a date once he transferred to another unit. He knew his feelings were real. She was the one for him. Maybe one day she would feel the same for him. Or maybe she already did.

Chapter 9

Today was the day that he had been waiting for a long. Sure, he had taken several other women, but he had saved the best for last. Grace was like a cherry on top for him. He had been watching his last seven women all month. Grace was one of them. He knew their daily routines like he knew the back of his hand. What they ate, drank, and even what they slept in. He chuckled to himself. There was only one that he really wanted under him, and he wanted her forever.

"Oh, my sweet, beautiful Grace. Daddy's coming for you, sweet girl. Daddy's coming."

Grace Green. The most beautiful girl in her lane. She had silky straight blonde hair and naturally pumped pink lips. She had an athletic body with her curves on point as she worked out daily. Daddy had been head over heels for Grace for some time now. Not because he loved her. Nope. He never loved anyone except Anna. But because he wanted her underneath him. He wanted to enjoy her. He had very prominent sexual feelings for her, unlike other girls he had kidnapped before.

Daddy saw Grace preparing herself for her morning jog. It was 6 am, and the sun was rising beautifully.

What a beautiful day to have you, dear Grace!

As she began her run, Daddy ran too behind her carefully. He did not want to get caught just now. He kept on following her. Daddy had a tough routine, so he was physically fit enough to catch up with Grace. After running for half an hour, at one point, Grace paused to catch her breath and drink water.

This was the golden chance. Daddy had to take this chance to kidnap her. It was now or never. There was no one around, and she was far away from anyone to hear her.

Daddy took his chance. He jumped right behind her and grabbed her from her back. His one hand held her mouth so that if she screamed, her voice doesn't get loud. His other hand held her by her waist. Grace tried to get away. She kept on hitting him with her feet, but nothing was working on him. He was standing still like a steel rod. Daddy wasn't struggling with Grace. He was taking his time with her.

Grace suddenly remembered she had kept a can of pepper spray with her before leaving her house. Since her hands were free, she was able to get hold of the pepper spray. She took it out and sprayed it back at him without seeing where she was spraying it. She missed Daddy's eyes because of her angle. Daddy got so angry with this act of Grace that he grabbed her tightly by her arms and threw her spray can away. He grabbed her tightly with one hand and pulled out his handkerchief that was already sprayed with Chloroform. Grace quickly understood the mess she had created. The way Daddy was holding her now was enough for her to realize he was angry now. He placed his handkerchief on her nose, and very easily, Grace lost her senses. She tried to fight him off but could not.

Daddy grabbed Grace and placed a pair of sunglasses on her eyes. It did not hint that she was unconscious. Daddy made her walk towards his car. Grace was not her senses, but she could still walk. Anyone who passed by her would either see her as a drunk girl returning from a late-night party or a sick girl trying to walk.

Daddy reached his SUV with Grace. He carefully made her sit in the front seat. Everyone saw him as someone who was taking care of her. They both looked like they were a couple. Daddy was angry with her, but he still handled her with care. She was making him feel hard even though he was only just handling her now. Daddy then sat on his seat and quickly but carefully left. He made sure it did not seem as if he was running away.

They were soon on the road. Daddy took Grace's fanny pack and, while driving, looked into it. The pack had a pink lipstick, Grace's cellphone, a deodorant, and an energy drink. Daddy took out her lipstick and her deodorant and threw away her pack. He did not want to leave any trace of her, but he also wanted to keep her lipstick so she could get ready for him.

Grace was Daddy's jackpot. While on their way to the barn, Daddy couldn't help but look at Grace as if he was scanning her. Very far away from where he kidnapped Grace, on the highway, Daddy stopped his car on the side of the road. He kept looking at Grace with all his might. His hand went inside Grace's shirt and pressed her breasts. He lifted up her shirt and took a good look. *"This is heaven"* Daddy slowly slides his hand into the waist of her exercise pants, carefully sliding his fingertips over the elastic of her panties. He could not control himself. Daddy had been sexually attracted to Grace since the moment he saw her. She was finally here with him now. He was having his moment. He was enjoying himself.

FOCUS! STUPID FOCUS!

Daddy suddenly realized his main task. He did not kidnap Grace for sex. He kidnapped Grace for his quota. He needs to take her to the barn as soon as possible. He must complete his quota. There he can have fun with her, but right now, he has to take her to her place.

Daddy quickly took out his hand from Grace's pants. And held on to the steering. *"Not a problem. Once we reach, you are all mine until someone buys you."* He drove towards the barn. *"I will make sure no one buys you so that you stay with me for some time. Give me the chance to enjoy all of you."*

Chapter 10

Jessica

Jessica had now started preparing herself to go undercover. She was changing everything about her appearance that she could. She booked an appointment to change her hairstyle.

It was 3 pm. Jessica entered the salon. She thumbed through the hairstyle magazine and looked through a couple of styles to choose from for a complete color and style change. She wanted something dangerous, different, yet simple. Something that was not her style.

"You can come on back. We are ready for you."

Jessica stands and walks to the back of the salon. Ready or not, here goes nothing. Jessica sits down.

"So? Were you able to decide what you want?"

"Yeah, I saw something in the magazine. I want your opinion on it too."

"Sure, what is it?"

Jessica pulls out the magazine and points it to the lady in the picture.

"I was thinking about a mixture of this style and this color. What do you think? How will this look on me?"

"It would look good. I am very sure, but that is totally different from what you have currently. Are you sure you want to go for that major change?"

"I am very positive. I want to walk out as a whole different person."

"Great! Then let's get started."

Jessica laid back in the chair as the stylist began her process of making her someone unrecognizable.

She chopped her hair off into a beautiful graduation bob and dyed them silver. She then went to the market and got herself contact lenses to wear in place of her glasses. She wanted to look different.

Jessica also got her new paperwork done.

"What is your name?" The man filling her ID asked.

"Sarah," she said.

"Full name please?"

"Sarah D' Cruz."

He filled out her documents and handed her her files. She was officially now Sarah D' Cruz.

She then found herself a new job as a real estate agent and also bought herself a suite to live in.

"You have a huge suite," people around her would say.

She did everything she could to depict the personality of a famous person to get good connections. She was meeting celebrities and politicians to keep herself upfront with the current news of the city. She also started visiting clubs and bars to keep a close look at people. These times she would not take her files with her, instead would go and buy her drinks but not drink to remain conscious. She started spending time with girls around to get to know good people.

"Oh my god! We love your personality, Sarah!" the girls would say.

Jessica was trying to give her best. She wanted to be all in. She wanted to spend enough time talking to girls to find out the details she needed. The girls would often gossip about that particular girl who left the bar with such a handsome boy.

"Oh, he had such a sharp jawline."

"And his eyes were sharp too."

"He looked like someone straight outta a movie."

The girls couldn't stop adoring him. Nobody knew his actual truth. Nobody knew what kind of person he was. They just knew what he looked like.

"You girls have no idea who you are looking at," Jessica would think.

Jessica going undercover was a secret. It was a secret only her partner, Agent Murphey, and her director knew. No one else knew how the investigation was escalating. While on her rounds with girls around the town, Jessica noticed that Daddy only targeted girls that were easy to catch or had any weak points. Some were either living alone, some were underage, and some were just easy.

Spending time like this was difficult for Jessica. She was out there without any support, all alone and with just one gun with her. Jessica was back into the streets like her past. In her past, she was unaware of the existence of the bad guys, so she lived a carefree life until she was kidnapped. Today, years later, she is aware of the bad guys. Thoughts about them are unsettling her.

Jessica still liked Robert, aka Daddy! She was insecure about how girls liked him, but at the same time, she was telling herself not to let her feelings control her. She did not want daddy to keep on doing want he was doing. She wanted to catch him and ask him why he did what he did.

"Why me, Robert?"

She kept herself hidden, but she also kept on working on her investigation. She did not want to ruin this very chance she had to catch him. she was confident, and she was very motivated. She knew what she had to do. Jessica was also scared, but she did not let her fear take over her profession and her purpose of finding the person who ruined her life and now is ruining other girls' life.

"Robert, you will go to hell. I will make sure about that."

Chapter 11

A new look, a new town, a new apartment, even a new identity. Jessica prides herself in this deep undercover world. Agent Murphy lived next door to Jessica. AKA Sarah D' Cruz. It was hard for Murphy to pretend he did not have this yielding love for Jessica as she lived her undercover life of Sarah. Only if Jessica knew how much her fellow agent really was in love with her. Agent Murphy was the sweetest, most loyal partner Jessica had ever had. And yet she was still unable to decode how much in love her agent was with her.

Agent Murphy was a very patient man. Surely, Jessica would see him for what he was. Surely, Jessica would see him for how much he was in love with her. He prayed for her every day. He read Bible verse after Bible verse, seeking answers as to why Jessica wasn't interested. He knew Jessica had Stockholm Syndrome, and that was hard to compete with. She was loving a man that was evil, and it was something he struggled to cope with. Him being passed over for a man who is several years older than him and listed on the international website for human trafficking was hard to swallow.

Murphy watched as Jessica walked out the door promptly at 5:30 am for her morning run. Choosing this time to run gave Daddy a chance to see her before the sun rose over the apartment buildings. Murphy waited approximately ten minutes before he walked out the door for his run as well. Choosing a crossing path but leaving Jessica to do her thing. They had been doing this same schedule for five months now, and there was no sign that daddy was anywhere near or that he was even interested in Jessica.

Murphy was happy that their boss had discussed pulling them from the assignment if Daddy didn't start paying her any attention. Especially with more girls going missing in various locations all around Jessica's age or younger.

Murphy passed Jessica on the right as their paths crossed, smiling at her and blowing her a kiss as couples would do. She blushed. Oblivious that murphy wasn't just acting. Ten more minutes, Jessica would have made her two-mile run lap back to the apartment. She stopped to stretch on the stairs as she waited for Murphy. Murphy came up beside her as she finished stretching, grabbing her around the waist. She smiled as he pulled her into a sweaty embrace. Playfully pushing him away as she took the stairs up to the apartment entrance. Dramatically waving him to follow.

In the shadows, Daddy watched her. He always watched her. He felt something familiar about her, but she was so close to his personal hometown that it was too risky to just snatch her as he had the others and that dang boyfriend of hers was always there. Doesn't he have a job?

Later that week, Murphy suggested that Jessica go down to the local Tavern to see if Daddy had shown up. He would remain behind but would be outside the Tavern just in case Daddy showed. After all, he knew that Jessica always managed to find herself in trouble.

Promptly at 5pm, Friday evening, Jessica walked into the Tavern. It was a ladies' night. It was still early, but this time frame allowed her to scope out the bar before it became crowded at 5:30 pm.

Free drinks were there all around. She walked into the bar and ordered a club soda. The bartender threw her a dirty look.

"Club soda, huh? I don't make money off club soda," The bartender stated rudely.

"Yeah, For now. I don't know what I want just yet." Jessica said shyly. She honestly didn't want to drink. She wanted to remain clear-headed if she was to catch this guy.

The bartender slammed the club soda down on the bar.

"I don't run a tab for bullshit. I'll need you to pay for your club soda."

"I thought the drinks were free tonight. You know, ladies' night."

"It is only selected drinks. That will be ten bucks."

"For a club soda?"

"Ten bucks or get out my bar."

Shocked, Jessica pulled a twenty out of her pocket and laid it on the bar. The bartender snatched it up as she walked away. Surprised by her attitude Jessica sipped the club soda. But the bartender had just ensured that if Daddy was in the bar, she was officially noticed. She pulled her lipstick and mirror out of her purse and pretended to apply another coat to her already gorgeous lips. Her manicured hands flashed in the light, with the diamond catching the light and sparkling as well.

The bartender called down from the register. "Thanks for the tip." As she looked at Jessica squarely in the eye.

"Dang, you pissed her off, huh?"

Jessica turned to see a handsome man not five feet from her. He smiled big, flashing his big blue eyes and bright white teeth. She knew instantly who she was staring at, and her heart raced. Her skin felt clammy, and she couldn't breathe. It felt as if time had stopped, or worse, she was dreaming!

She laughed nervously. "I guess so."

He flashed another smile at her. "Would you like another drink?"

"Not yet. I don't think she is quite over me ordering this one yet." Jessica laughed at her own sarcastic comment. She wasn't sure how to work this now that she was face to face with the man they were after. Her insecurities were obvious to her but maybe not to him.

Tonight, he wore a white shirt, unbuttoned at the neck. His blazer hung loosely and open. His grey slacks were perfectly hemmed with his black loafers. He wore a gold Rolex on his left wrist. She noted quickly as being an indicator that he was right-handed. He wore no wedding ring or other jewelry. His eyes were blue against his dark hair. It then instantly clicked with her. He had changed his hair color. His haircut wasn't a tight military type of cut. It had grown out past his ears.

"Want to hit the dance floor?" He asked casually

"Uhm, maybe later. Tell me about yourself?"

"Isn't nothing much to tell, sweetheart. Just do some meager selling for a living. And come here and try to unwind from the week."

"That sounds like the perfect life."

"What do you do for a living? Tell me about your beautiful eyes."

Jessica took a deep breath. She had rehearsed this a million times. She could feed him the lie they had practiced over and over.

"Just a girl getting away for a night without her boyfriend in town. I work in real estate, and I am a photographer by passion and just freelance since he travels all the time."

Jessica suddenly felt her nerves getting the best of her. She felt nauseous.

"I'm sorry, I must go to the restroom. Would you excuse me?"

As Jessica went to stand, she swayed. The stranger's arms went around her waist to steady her.

"I'm good." She stated hastily as she pulled out of his embrace. Determined to walk out alone.

Her heart raced. Her body betrayed her mind as things became fuzzy. Her hand went to her forehead. How did he do this? She was about to be kidnapped again.

Murphy. She thought briefly as she felt Daddy pull her back by his side.

"Let me take you home," he said slyly. As he pulled her toward the exit. This was getting easier and easier, Daddy thought to himself. As he walked with Jessica out of the Tavern.

Chapter 12

Murphy sat outside the Tavern, watching the entrance that doubled as the exit. It was still early, and he didn't expect Jessica for at least another two hours. He had no idea what she did in there for several hours as she always came out sober and not a hair out of place. The Tavern was known for its karaoke, so maybe that's what she did those several hours. He would sure love to hear her sometime if so. His mind drifted to the songs she would sing as he caught a glimpse of what appeared to be Jessica only. She was being held up by a gentleman that was breathtakingly handsome, even to him, a heterosexual male.

Then it hit him. All these months had finally paid off. Jessica had caught the attention of Daddy again.

He watched for a moment. CRAP!!!! He hit the steering wheel. She had let him drug her.

He grabbed his cell phone and called the director.

The phone rang for what seemed like forever. He continued to watch Daddy and Jessica. They were 100ft from the corner where he would lose sight.

DANG, ANSWER THE PHONE! He screamed in his mind.

"Palmer, what you got, Murphy. "

"About time, Palmer. What I have is Daddy with Jessica, and in 75 feet, I will lose complete sight of them. Please advise?"

"Pursue. Do not engage!" Palmer advised. As he simultaneously called the local folks in the small town of Sylvester, Georgia. Where he had already advised the local Sheriff of their presence and belief that Daddy was working closely in the area. Of Course, the Sheriff didn't believe him. Because he was a small quiet town. These country boys never believed what was happening right under their own noses. If Murphy would pursue it, they could find the place where Ash kept the girls. He just had to do this right. Palmer knew Murphy's feelings about Jessica were intense. Sometimes, these long undercover assignments made your heart play tricks on you.

"Son of a biscuit eater nose picking lying cracker jack!" Palmer said to no one as he reached the Sheriff's voicemail. "Murphy update?"

"They have just got into Jessica's FBI-issued undercover car, Black Honda, License plate ISBA 9781. She is in the passenger seat. She appears to have been drugged. As she came out of the Tavern."

"On it, " Palmer stated as he instructed the rest of the team to begin tracking her car. As he used his other phone to radio into the team. "Team, Palmer immediate APB out on ISBA 9781 Operated by Agent Jessica Lee. The last location is Tavern 101 N Isabella Street in Sylvester, Georgia. Subject was last seen with a man of interest, Robert Ash, also known as, Daddy. Consider armed and dangerous do not approach. Follow closely. I repeat, do not apprehend the suspect."

"Update Murphy."

"Following at a safe distance. Subject just made a right turn onto Isabella Street, currently stopped at the red light on Isabella and Highway 82. Subject is in the left turning lane."

"Murphy, don't lose them. Follow protocol. Don't let your emotions take over."

"Sheriff, finally. This is Agent Palmer. We have a situation. Robert Ash, wanted for several ongoing investigations of a missing woman, is currently in possession of one of our agents."

Palmer listened to the Sheriff offer his services in any way he could, of course, be of service.

Murphy could only hear one side of the conversation, but his heart raced. He never thought that Ash would come this close to his home address. Let alone take Jessica again.

"Murphy, listen up the team is five minutes out to take over the situation so that you can come in and debrief. Our goal is to apprehend when they get to the location where Ash is keeping the girls.

"I CAN'T JUST LEAVE JESSICA TO FEND FOR HERSELF," Murphy shouted into the phone.

It was just what Palmer was expecting from him. That is what happens when you feel in emotional love with your partner. You become blinded by that emotion and unable to think past it.

Just then, a blue SUV pulled out in front of Murphy from a side road. Murphy hadn't even noticed. When he got around the SUV, Jessica's Honda was gone.

Murphy hit the steering wheel again as tears slide down his cheeks. Grown men weren't supposed to cry. But, son of a biscuit eater, he had just lost his partner, and now she was in the hands of her kidnapper. She wasn't going to be so lucky twice.

Chapter 13

Daddy and Jessica left the club together. Jessica guided Daddy to her car. She was drunk yet she managed to stay on the plan. As soon as Jessica tried to sit on the driver's seat, she stumbled upon it.

"Do you need help?" asked Daddy.

"No! I'm perfectly fine!" she replied.

"Let me help you."

Daddy helped Jessica get out of her car and took her to her passenger seat. Then he went to the driver's seat and took Jessica's car from the parking lot to the main road.

When driving, Daddy noticed a car following his car from way behind, from since when he left with Jessica in her car. Daddy wasn't stupid. He knew something was up. There were three theories in his mind; (1) They were being chased because of Daddy. (2) Jessica was someone important and she had a protocol. (3) Someone was actually following them. Either way, Daddy was doomed. Jessica was passed out in her passenger seat. Daddy grabbed her purse and took out her identification card.

JESSICA

INVESTIGATION DEPARTMENT

"Bullseye! I knew something was up! At least don't carry your ID card along with you, you stupid lady!" Daddy thought to himself.

Stressed, Daddy tried to figure out the motion of the car behind him.

"You are a challenge, Jessica. I love challenges."

Daddy was smart, he decided to take Jessica to her house. Luckily, Jessica's car had a GPS system. It had her house address saved in it. Daddy turned the map on the car's screen and started tracking Jessica's way home. Daddy did not want to risk any of the operations. His operation of completing his quota and the operation of the person his car behind. He didn't try to speed up or confuse the tail following him, instead he as a perfect gentleman dropped Jessica home. It was ruining his plans but anything was better than getting caught. The car took him to Jessica's house. He carefully parked her car and ran away in a flash.

Daddy left his impression of the nice gentleman, left Jessica with questions when she wakes up and also he got away with his identification. He lost the tail four blocks ago so he was pretty sure that they would not catch him running from her apartment. Daddy knew something was up. He knew he had to be more careful now. His identity was in danger now. Maybe because they have been asking for too many girls now. The quota had been increasing lately, which means increase in kidnapping. Maybe that's why it is now more noticeable for the police. The complaints might have increased.

"I will talk to them about getting calm with the quota," thought Daddy. "They don't realize what trouble they are putting me and themselves into."

Jessica was left in her car. It was parked in her apartment with the windows halfway down to left air pass through and she was able to breath. Daddy wanted his complete, good image of a gentleman so he went to his extremes.

The car following Daddy and Jessica finally reached to Jessica's apartment. They saw Jessica in the car, passed out and the car is parked safely.

Chapter 14

Murphy called into dispatch just to ensure that someone was trying to tail Jessica's Honda. He hated being called off. He was angry and tempted to just go home and crash. It always felt like the devil tugging at him to grab a six-pack and drink his cares away. He knew from a lifelong time of being the person that alcohol controlled that it wasn't the way to solve his problem. So, he took the turn for their undercover rental apartment. After all, it was what he was supposed to do.

Murphy turned on the street that the apartment complex was on. He rounded the corner; he could see the company-issued Honda.

"Holy Crap!" He whispered to no one in particular.

Should he drive by? Where was Daddy? Was Jessica in the car? Inside with Daddy? Images ran through his mind.

He was scared for Jessica. His training took over as he cruised by the Honda a safe distance before turning into a parking spot further up.

"Dispatch, this is Murphy."

"Agent, I thought our orders were clear. You were to return to your apartment and await further instructions."

"Oh, I am home, but so is Jessica's car."

Dispatch radios back quickly for him not to enter the residence. As if he was going to wait on someone else to find Jessica. He got out of the truck and walked quickly to the side of the apartment, trying to hide yet peer into the Honda at the same time. The Honda was empty except for the passenger side.

There sat Jessica with her head tilted to the side. She looked like she was sleeping peacefully. Jessica was in her car, comfortable yet passed out. Skipping protocol, he ran to the passenger door, yanking it open. Who cared if his fingerprints were all over the car and covered the kidnappers. He had to get to Jessica.

Nothing mattered. Not the case. Not Robert Ash. Nothing. Just Jessica. Murphy reached out to open her door. She had the seat belt on and was safe. He checked her pulse just as he heard the sirens getting closer. She was still alive. He felt the breath he was holding released in a rush, almost causing him to lose his balance as his sight went blurry.

"Really? He just left her here in the most comfortable and safe position. I don't believe it!" said Murphy, but no one was around to hear him.

All Murphy wanted was for Jessica to be okay. He tried to take care of her as he was deeply in love with her. Looking at Jessica like that, his heart was beating so fast. She looked so beautiful as he looked at her. Murphy had mixed emotions. He was angry and stressed.

Why? Why did you have to do this? Why are you so eager to prove yourself? You should know I trust you.

He was angry at her for going undercover, but he couldn't say this to her.

Why her always? What to do? I can't lose her. I can't. Even if she doesn't acknowledge it.

He was stressed because she was in such a position. He wanted to protect her. She meant the world to him.

Daddy! I'm going to make sure you die in prison!

Chapter 15

Daddy could not believe what he just did. he was constantly questioning himself.

"Did I, Daddy, just drop a gorgeous lady home? Instead of taking her with me, did I really? What's wrong with me?"

Daddy knew it was not because of him. It was because of her she made him do it. She made him feel weak on his nerves. Daddy decides to look for her. He really wants to meet the woman who made Daddy so gentle. No one has ever been able to do that. No one.

"Jessica, I'm coming for you."

Daddy decides to look for Jessica.

Walking up the stairs to the attic, Daddy paused to look at himself in the mirror. He should not be doing this. He should leave the past in the past, he thought to himself. His body betrayed him as he continued up the stairs.

He unlocked the attic door and pushed it open. Walking into memory lane.

The box was labeled Anna, His first high school crush. Lifting the lid, he found folded handwritten letters with his name scribbled in child-like handwriting. He picked one up and opened it. It was from a much simpler time.

"My dearest Robert, I had so much fun last night walking by moonlight next to the creek. I love you so much and can't wait till we grow up and get married. I love you - Anna.

The next box was of his parents. He moved it to the side. Nothing he wanted to reminisce about today. Moving a couple of more boxes with stuff from his childhood. He came to the box marked "x" this was where he kept the small keepsakes, he kept from each of the girls he kidnapped.

He lifted the top off the box. His first box contained the first one hundred girls that he kidnapped. Each with a photo and a lock of hair. He thumbed through the photos until he found the one he was looking for.

Jessica Lee.

He pulled the picture out and smelled the hair as if her scent would remain.

His mind traveling back to a time when he thought he would be free of this life.

There she was young and beautiful. Blonde with a deep dark bronze tan. She was full of life. Laughing with her friends. She never screamed when he grabbed her, never fought back.

To him, her kidnapping was easier than any of the others.

Daddy went to a flower shop, bought a few white roses, and made a bouquet. Then he went to his nearest chocolate shop to get a box of chocolates. He then sat in his car and drove to Jessica's apartment.

Daddy parked his car in the next lane. He kept the roses, and the chocolates on Jessica's doorstep rang the bell and ran like a maniac toward his car. When Jessica came out, she didn't see him there.

Daddy wants to impress Jessica. He wants her to know who he is. The very same day when he sent her gifts, he saw her leave with a little suitcase. After that, she never returned. He kept on visiting her house and waited there for hours and hours on his every visit. There was no sign of her again.

Jessica had left that apartment as soon as she was suspended from her mission. She used to live in this apartment when she went undercover in search of Daddy.

One day, Daddy noticed that one of Jessica's windows was not locked. He opened that window and went inside her house. It was almost empty, but she still had a few of her clothes and basic essentials. Daddy went to her closet and smelled every single dress hanging in the cupboard.

"It smells so familiar and breathtaking."

He stays in there for an hour. Lays down on her bed and tries to smell her completely and imagine her. How beautiful she looked. Her mesmerizing eyes, her shiny hair, her soft skin. Daddy tried to recall everything he could about Jessica.

"No, I don't drop everyone home, baby!"

Daddy wasn't even focusing on completing his quota. He wanted Jessica badly.

Days passed by of Daddy visiting Jessica's apartment in hopes of smelling her and finding her one day. He was behaving like a complete lunatic.

One day, as daddy lay on Jessica's couch, he heard the door cling. The door was getting unlocked. He quickly ran into the guest room and closed the door. He left the door open just right enough for him to see who was entering. He saw a few police officers entering. These police officers seemed like they were searching the house.

"Search operation in an investigation department member, ironic."

Suddenly he heard whispers.

"Is he in here?"

"I don't think he would be in here."

Daddy instantly knew they were talking about him.

"Let's search the entire apartment."

Daddy froze.

It took him some time to get back to his senses. Then he realized he needed to hide or run away. He opens the door of the washroom slowly and looks for the window.

Perfect!

He struggles to unlock the window, and as soon as he does, it makes a loud cracking noise. This gets the policemen's attention. They enter the guest room quickly and start banging on the washroom door to break it open. Till the time they broke the lock and entered, daddy was standing on the window.

As they opened the door, they saw daddy jumping from the window. They jumped behind him, but they were not as smart as daddy. Daddy started running on his feet. The policemen followed him. Little did they know that daddy had years of training and was physically fit. They cannot run as much and as fast as daddy can. They lost him while he ran. He was too quick for them.

Daddy, when he reached home, couldn't stop thinking about him. Daddy knew something was wrong with him. He barely ditched the police who had staked out to find him.

"How did they know I might be here? Did someone see me? Did someone tell them? Why were they even here? Where is my love, Jessica?"

Daddy paused after a few blocks. To his surprise, he saw Jessica there. He watched her walk out of the Target store, phone in hand. She was with someone. They were laughing together and looking at their phones. They never looked when he approached them. He asked for help because his car would not start. He just wanted to use one of their phones. Whichever was nice enough to give him her phone would be the one that he took.

Jessica stopped immediately and walked toward him. His smile brightened the parking lot. She had never seen eyes so blue. It was as if her heart had stopped beating, and her lungs had forgotten how to breathe.

Chapter 16

Jessica is still laying in her car, passed out. Murphy picks Jessica up from the passenger seat and locks her car. Surprisingly she was light for him. She looked beautiful. Murphy had wanted to pick her up for so long and make love to her, but unfortunately, it had to be in such a situation when she was not in her consciousness. Murphy loved her, but she was too much into her kidnapper that Murphy never expressed his feelings.

Agent Murphy turns around and lays Jessica down on the concrete parking lot. He let her have fresh air in hopes that she would get up. At that moment, the EMS arrived on the scene, and also the authorities arrived at the same time. Director's assistant got furious when he saw that Murphy had removed Jessica and he was caressing her head. Boss was going to have his head for this one. He was strictly asked not to go near the car.

"How did you find her?" asked the authorities.

"She was in the car, sir," answered Murphy.

"Were you not instructed to not go near the car?"

"I was, yes, sir. But I did it only so that she could get fresh air and breath."

"…and you can caress her while she's unconscious?"

"No, sir. That was not my intention," replied Murphy with embarrassment.

As the officer and Agent Murphy were talking, the medical team was looking after Jessica. Thankfully enough, there was a medical team in the first place. Otherwise, in Murphy's previous department, there wasn't one.

"What's the update?" asked the officer to the medical team. "How is she doing?"

"Sir, we think we should take her to the hospital. It is better to keep her under observation," replied one of the medical team members.

"Is it something serious?" asked Agent Murphy.

"No, there is nothing to be worried about. We just need to do a few tests and make sure she is doing fine."

"Oh."

"Do you think she might be drugged?" asked the officer.

"We doubt so. Can only confirm when the test results are there."

"Sure. Take her in the van to the hospital."

Looking at Murphy, the officer knew he wanted to go along with her.

"Go with her, Murphy," he said with a little smile.

Agent Murphy watched the medical team load Jessica into the van. She was still unconscious and needed to get done with a few tests. They wanted to be sure that if she had been drugged by Daddy, her body would get rid of it.

"Murphy, me sending you with her doesn't mean I have become soft to you. She needs you. That's the only reason why. You will still see me tomorrow. Good luck with it," said the officer.

"But what did I do?"

"You know it well what you just did. That's what you get when you don't listen to your higher ones."

Murphy knew he wasn't allowed any contact with Jessica. Still, he went for it. Murphy might be on the edge of losing his job, but with love comes great sacrifices. He stayed back to take care of her, and he wanted Jessica to wake up as soon as possible. He wanted her to acknowledge him and his efforts for her.

Jessica was loaded into the bed in the van. She had a small bottle of an antibiotic to stop her from getting weak. She was needed badly by Murphy. Nobody knows what will happen tomorrow, but all Murphy knows is that Jessica will be better than today.

Jessica, my dear, I love you so much. I will not let anything happen to you. I will protect you.

Chapter 17

Jessica spent the entire week in the hospital. She was under observation and undergoing tests. The tests did find out that she was drugged by Daddy, and the drug he used was a little heavy but not harmful.

Jessica was soon discharged. Agent Murphy took her to her apartment to rest and settle down. She was not a fan of hospitals and badly wanted to go home. She goes home, freshens herself, and goes to sleep on her comfortable bed. However, agent Murphy doesn't leave her alone. He stayed in her apartment to look after her if she needed any help.

The next day, Jessica wakes up. She finds Agent Murphy sleeping on her couch and wakes him up.

"Murphy, Murphy," Jessica tries to wake Murphy softly, but he doesn't wake up.

She goes to her kitchen and makes coffee for herself to wake herself up. Then she goes to freshen herself up. In the meantime, murphy wakes up.

"Oh hey, good morning," said Jessica.

"Hello, good morning. How are you feeling?" asked Murphy.

"Perfectly fine!"

"That's great! I have a few questions for you."

"Wait, let me pour you some coffee first."

"Sure."

Jessica and Murphy did not get enough time to talk about the details. Jessica heads back to her kitchen and makes coffee for Murphy. She then brings it to him and sits beside him on the couch.

"Jess, who was it? Why did you leave with him?"

"You won't believe me, but it was Daddy. It was him. I saw Robert!"

"How are you so sure?"

"I remember those eyes. I remember that fragrance."

Agent Murphy sighed.

"What is the last thing that you remember?"

"The last thing I remember is that I drank and walked out with Daddy."

"Well, I was right behind tracing you. he dropped you here in your parking lot, and when I got here, he was gone."

"You are kidding me! I clearly looked like his next target."

"Maybe he found out?"

"Maybe."

Jessica and murphy chatted for some time, and then murphy left for his home.

Later that evening, Jessica's doorbell rang. As she opened the door, there was no one out there but a bouquet of flowers and a box of chocolates at her doorstep. It had a name tag on it, "JESSICA."

Jessica took them in. She placed them on her table while constantly staring at the name tag.

"Who could have sent these? Did Murphy? No, I don't think so. Who else, then?"

She turned the card and was shocked to see what was written on it.

"FROM D."

"D? Who's initial is D?"

She suddenly realized that Daddy had seen her address when he dropped her home.

"Is it Daddy? No way!"

She quickly calls Murphy and tells him everything.

"Jess, I think for now you should pack everything important that needs to be carried and come to my place. We will then talk to the Director when he's back in the office."

Jessica agrees to his idea and packs everything she needs.

When the Director comes back to his office, Jessica and Murphy rush to meet him. Jessica sits across from her boss. They discuss everything with him.

"Jessica, I think the best solution to this is that you should stop being undercover," says the Director. "Already you are on medical leave. You should take a rest."

"Are you trying to say that I am suspended? No! I don't think that's necessary," resists Jessica.

"Call it whatever you want to call it, but you are done. At least until the doctor clears you. Murphy, please try to explain it to her. It is dangerous for her to continue."

"I think the Director is right. You need to back off from the operation. It is important for you. You will end up getting yourself in danger," said Murphy.

"Jessica, I'm sorry, but I will have to suspend you from the operation. I am placing you in a secure house, you and Murphy both. This is not up for discussion. Get your stuff. You have an hour."

"Please, this is my only chance."

"I think this will help you mentally, too, with the feeling of being followed. Don't forget you are his next target. We will help you change your identity, and you will have guards assigned to you for your protection. It will only be for a few days."

"Jessica, please, I think it's for your own good. Just for some time," pleaded Murphy.

She gave it a thought. She knew she had to find Daddy, but she also had to go by the Director and Murphy. She ends up agreeing with the Director's offer. What if she is able to find something? Jessica rose from her seat and walked to the door. She looked back at her boss. "This isn't over," she says as she opens the door, letting it slam as she walks out.

Chapter 18

Jessica was furious about her suspension. She couldn't believe that she had been removed from the undercover mission.

Why do they underestimate me? Why don't they understand that this mission is very important to me?

Jessica did not want to be placed in the safe house. Instead, she wanted her to work.

Safe House? No way that's happening! Over my dead body!

She had to catch this Piece of Stew. She had to save the other women. She grabbed her car keys out of her purse. It was given to her by the FBI department. It screamed the government from a mile away.

Unlocking the doors with the key fob, as soon as she opens the door, she gets surprised to find Murphy already sitting in the passenger seat, waiting for her.

"OMG! You almost killed me, Murphy! What are you doing here?" she asks him.

"Here for the same reason that you are here for, going to a safe house," he says with a smile.

"No sir, I am going to catch this POS, and I don't need your help."

"Jessica, he got you the second time. Do you understand the sensitivity of the situation? Anything can happen to you. So the third time, do you want us to find you dead?"

"Better dead with answers than alive hiding in fear." She smirked at him. "I can't live like this, hiding, looking over my shoulder. He wasn't going to hurt me. He had no idea who I was. You know about everything, Murphy."

Murphy laughed. "NO idea who you were, then explain why the contents of your glove box and purse were dumped out in the driver's seat. And why on earth would you carry your original FBI id on you on an undercover mission?"

"He was just looking for something. Maybe he just dropped something."

"Jessica, wake up. You are not this stupid. What is it about this guy that makes you blind?"

"He took years of my life I can't get back, and that should be enough reason to want to see him behind bars."

"It is more than that, though, and you know it."

"You do not know anything about me or how I feel. Now get out of my car. I have things to do."

"I am not leaving you. We are going to the safe house. You have thirty minutes, and we have a tail."

Murphy emphasized tail when he turned his head to the back of the car to see three more agents on each side of the car.

"Ugh... Y'all are ridiculous." Jessica said, slamming the car door shut.

Jessica was not joking around. If the FBI doesn't let her find him, then she will find him on her own. She was not settling down on anything less. She wanted to know him badly.

Robert, you can't get away from me! Even if it means leaving the FBI. I will find you at any cost.

Chapter 19

Agent Murphy sat in the car, looking in disbelief as Jessica slammed the door. The other agents watching her were just as shocked as he was. He wasn't sure rather to follow her or let her calm down. She wasn't thinking rationally.

Robert knew her real identity, and not only that, but he also knew where she lived. Murphy couldn't see all this. It was creating rage in him. He loved Jessica and wanted to take care of her, but Jessica kept on resisting to go and search for Daddy. She is in love with her kidnapper, and she doesn't understand the trouble she is putting herself into.

In anger, Murphy hit the dashboard with his fist, causing a sharp pain to run up his arm. Also causing his assigned agent to look at him through the window. He never would get used to having someone follow him. But until Robert was caught, this was going to be life.

How do I make her understand that she is putting herself into trouble? How do I tell her about my feelings? How do I let her know that she needs to take care of herself? How is she so sure that Daddy won't harm her the next time he finds her?

Jessica was never going to listen to Murphy. She would still do what she wanted to do. Murphy was stuck with her just as much as she was stuck with him, rather either of them liked it or not. The quicker Jessica accepted that the quicker the team could find Robert and arrest him. Jessica wanted to do everything on her own. She needs to understand it is more teamwork than it is an individual mission. She will eventually need her team members to back up for her up whenever she would be in trouble.

Chapter 20

Jessica was fighting mad. *How dare the bureau think that they could send me off to some safe house?* This guy just drugged her again. Tried to take her off for the second time in her life.

She was not stopping until he was caught and put behind bars so that he is never able to hurt anyone again. Even if that catch costs her her life. And according to everyone, including Murphy, that is just what it would cost her. But it did not matter to her. She was just thinking of all the women she could save, even if saving them can cost her her life.

She continued to stomp off in the direction of the apartment that the bureau had rented for her under her assumed name. She needed to see it for herself before she headed to where she believed that Robert's home base was.

She hoped that he had left some sort of clue in her apartment that the crime unit had missed. It was a slim chance, but it was the only chance she had to know if she was really was in danger. According to the reports, nothing was missing inside from her home when the team went looking for Daddy. Nothing is in shambles. Did he really run away right after parking? Did he plan to bring her home the whole time? Was he even the man they had been chasing all along? Or was he just some man in the wrong place at the wrong time?

She walked into the apartment and looked around. Nothing seemed out of place. She went to the bedroom, and again nothing was out of place. She looked into her purse, noting the contents of her wallet shoved loosely into the bottom of it. Her actual identification was laid on top as if placed purposefully there.

Murphy was right. He knew who she was. He knew how to get to her no matter where she went. And for that reason alone, she couldn't go to the safe house.

She walked out the back door to the only place that Robert could be hiding. If she was caught by her assigned agent, she would be screwed. So, she stuck to the shadows of the alley as she headed toward the bus stop that would take her to the small town outside of Arlington.

She walked to the closet, where she kept her private notes on this case and things she had never shared with anyone. It included things she remembered about her time in captivity.

She grabbed the notebook, shoved clothes in a bag, and headed out of the apartment. She knew just where Robert would be and just how to get him to come in all by himself.

Chapter 21

"Robert Ash, we have you surrounded. Come out with your hands up." Jessica shouted outside the door of the country home.

Robert had to come out of his own free will. Jessica didn't have the place surrounded. No one even knew where she was. She had followed a hunch and nothing more. Venturing out on her own. She laughed to herself. She wasn't even supposed to be in today. If this went wrong, who would know?

She had managed to lose herself in the Tavern in Orlando, Florida. Nine hundred miles outside her jurisdiction. She followed Daddy all the way back into South Georgia. She was standing outside his home at 12:35, Oak Valley in Arlington. A huge country home faced her.

"Robert! Come out with your hands up. We have you surrounded."

Silence greeted her.

She knew he had to be there. She followed the car to the drive. Choosing to pull further down the road and come in on foot had only taken a few extra minutes. She could still see the driveway. No one could get in or out without her seeing them. The path that she had followed was at the entrance of the main drive.

Jessica pushed the door ever so gently as it squeaked on its rusty hinges. She paused, waiting for a noise other than that of her own breathing.

She further pushed the door and walked inside. Keeping her gun pointed straight ahead, she began to move along the wall. Slowly clearing every room. She made her way to the staircase. Climbing the stairs slowly, her eyes scanning the room. Her gun focused on the landing at the top of the staircase. Her mind screamed for her to stop and turn around. Just call this in. Get the cavalry coming. Her stomach turned and twisted as she made it to the landing.

She paused briefly, following the muffled sounds coming from further down the hall. Her gun pointed toward the door.

"Hello, Jessica. I have been expecting you."

Jessica turned toward the voice. Looked into the brownest eyes and immediately knew she stood face-to-face with Robert Ash.

"Stay where you are." She pointed the gun toward his torso. "Robert Ash, I am here to take you into custody for trafficking women."

"No, you aren't."

"There is a whole swat team waiting for me to tell them to come in."

"No, there isn't," Robert flashed his pearly whites in a smile. "It is just you, Jessie, my Jessie girl."

"I am not your Jessie. Now turn around and put your hands on your head."

"Now, now, Jessie. You finally connected the dots to right back where your nightmare started. Face to face with the man that haunts your dreams at night. Just put your weapon down and come on over to Daddy."

Robert took a slight step forward. Jessie took a slight step backward, her gun still aimed at him.

"Last warning Robert Ash, you are under arrest. Raise your hands above your head and place them on top of your head."

"Now, Jessie, we both know who gives the orders in this house. I want you to place your gun back in its holster and step closer to me."

Jessica hesitated. His voice caught her off guard. It was soothing to hear.

"Jessie, I know you remember my touch and how my breath felt on your ear and neck. How my lips felt as I kissed you."

"You're under arrest. Let's go." Jessica's voice quivered.

Robert continued speaking. "How I felt when I entered you."

"Just stop, stop. You're going to jail!" Her voice quivered again as Robert took another step forward until he was face-to-face within inches of her. Tears streamed down her face. Her tough girl act is gone.

Reaching to take Jessica's gun out of her hand. Dropping it to the ground as he bent down to kiss her. He felt her melt into his rough embrace.

"Shh! Shh! It's okay, my girl. Daddy's got you."

Chapter 22

He had reported Jessica missing from the safe house several hours ago. He had been searching for hours, going over leads that they had discussed over the course of the case. He had traveled over two hundred miles in one day. This was the last place he thought she could possibly be. Especially if Robert had her again.

Murphy rounded the corner to find Jessica in the arms of Robert Ash. He pulls his gun from his holster, taking aim at Robert.

He should just pull the trigger and take the consequences for killing the man.

Murphy crouched down out of sight. Silently praying that the calvary would be coming around the corner any moment now.

Listening closely, he only heard the whistle of the wind as it blew through the trees of the pecan orchard behind him. Could he signal Jessica? Let her know she was not alone.

He watched as what appeared to be a romantic conversation took place. He could faintly hear Robert's voice over his own breathing.

"Jessica, just come with me. I love you. It has always been you."

"Why did you turn me lose all those years ago?"

"I told you, Jessie, it was because I could not sell the woman I loved."

"You don't love me. You raped me. You kidnapped me. You took years of my life and held me in captivity. That isn't love."

"But it is. Jessie, I set you free so you could grow up. So that one day we could be together."

"And the other girls, where are they?"

"Gone, Jessie. There are no other girls. It will just be you and I when I take you back."

"The other girls, Robert. Where are they?"

"The shipment just shipped out on the container vessel. Half will make it to their destination, and some won't. However, the ones that went for good money are already with their buyers on some private yacht or plane out of the United States now."

Murphy listened as Robert kept talking. Taking notes as he described which girls were on the container ship. He just wanted to end this sorry excuse for a human's life and spare the citizens the time and money to put him away.

Murphy stilled at the thought of honestly killing a man out of rage. Rage that he felt right now pouring through his body. He could just sight him in on the gun and pull the trigger. A quick, painless way to go when you don't know what hit you.

"Stop it, Murphy," he told himself. This is not how you were raised. This is not what you believe. You believe in the Justice of the United States. You believe in all humans having the right to a fair trial and a chance to repent of their sins to Jesus Christ. You cannot take that away from the man standing before you because he holds the woman you love.

The spiritual conflict was real. As he tossed words of wisdom and hate back and forth in his mind. A portion wanting to witness the man that held Jessica. While the other wished a painful death upon him. He could not take much more of this.

He turned to look back at Robert and Jessica. Just as a slight movement caught his attention on his right side. He slowly pulled his gun away from Robert as he turned toward the movement. Only to see a deer standing two feet away from him, looking curious yet not coming closer. Murphy exhaled in relief. They were pretty sure Robert worked alone. But he was a bit jumpy seeing how backup still had not arrived.

He crouched down, moving closer to Robert and Jessica. Just as the deer decided to jump out into the open, almost allowing Murphy to be seen. He watched Jessica and Robert turn fastly toward him. As the deer bounced out where he could be clearly seen. Stupid deer, he thought to himself.

Just as shots rang out toward him and the doe. Murphy crouched lower, sure that his cover wasn't blown, but returning gunfire would definitely make Robert aware he was no longer alone.

Aiming toward Robert Murphy rang out two shots. Clipping Robert in his right side and arm. Murphy watched as the gun slipped from Robert's hand as he tried to raise it again to fire back at Murphy. Jessica drops to the ground instead of taking cover. *What the....* He thought to himself as he fired off another shot toward Robert. Watching Robert fall back as he took the shot to his shoulder.

Murphy trotted closer as he watched Jessica pick the gun up and aim toward him.

"It's me, Jessie. It is me." Murphy shouted to her as she raised the gun.

"Why did you have to shoot him she shouted?" Her voice quivered. As she held the gun aimed at Murphy.

"Jessica, it's me. Murphy. Your partner. Put the gun down. You are safe." He shouts as he hears sirens coming closer. "Listen to me," Murphy pleaded in his head as he heard car doors begin to slam and the beating of steps as SWAT moved into place. Robert lay still on the pavement, inches away from Jessica, as she continued to hold the gun pointed in Murphy's direction.

"Drop it, Jessica!" Murphy pleaded again just as the SWAT commander came within his preferential vision.

"You shot him, Murphy. You shot him." Jessica cried as she began lowering the gun.

Murphy turned to see the SWAT team running around, quickly getting into place. This situation was escalating quickly. Jessica was an agent. But on suspension. And with that information and the current situation, this could turn ugly quickly.

Murphy lowered his head. He was exhausted. Clearly, this was going nowhere. And with the SWAT team here, this could go south in a hurry.

Chapter 23

Daddy was shot. He could hear Jessie and some guy name Murphy shouting back and forth as he began to fade in and out of consciousness. He sounded like he loved her as he pleaded for them to put the gun down. Daddy hoped she would shoot the guy for interrupting him. But his mind was starting to play tricks on him. He could hear his mother calling him. He could hear his father bellowing out Amazing Grace. He missed them so much. He shook his head to clear the memory, but the voice of his mother stayed.

He was either losing it completely or dying. Either way was not a great option. Surely, if he was dying, he would be on the quickest path to hell, especially for his actions.

Robert closed his eyes. He could clearly see mum. Standing there in her ankle-length dress.

"Robert. This lifestyle of yours is too much. It is not how we raised you. Robert. You hurt those girls. You sell those girls. Leaving their families to wonder if they are dead. And the ones that do die. Their families were left with nothing, no closure. I raised you better than that, young man. You forgot God, who is the most important.'

"Mum, I tried not to forget God, but it was just too much. My lifestyle is different than what you wanted for me. I love GOD, but I have things to do because of promises I made."

"Boy, you don't love God. You don't even know Him."

"Mum, you are dead, you are only in my head, and you have no idea who I know or don't know."

"Am I, son?"

Just as Robert was about to answer, his mum's voice disappeared. He was brought back to the reality of the cold hard ground. He could hear shouts around him. His mother's words echoed in his head.

"You don't know God."

Robert thought over the past eighteen years and all of the women he kidnapped and cared for before he sold them to the highest bidder. A wave of guilt washed over him. His mom was right. He didn't know God. He only knew of God. And obviously, there was a huge difference in that. He had felt so empty for so long, thinking it was because he had lost his family and Anna. But it wasn't that at all. It was because he had lost himself on his way. He had done many things wrong and also lost his religion on the way. There was only one way to fix that. He had to live.

Made in the USA
Columbia, SC
30 March 2023